bad machinery

THE CASE OF THE TEAM SPIRIT

AN ONI PRESS PUBLICATION

bad machinery

THE CASE OF THE TEAM SPIRIT

by
John Allison

Original edition edited by
James Lucas Jones & Jill Beaton

Pocket edition edited by
Ari Yarwood

Designed by
Hilary Thompson

PUBLISHED BY ONI PRESS INC.

publisher, **Joe Nozemack**

editor in chief, **James Lucas Jones**

v.p. of marketing & sales, **Andrew McIntire**

sales manager, **David Dissanayake**

publicity coordinator, **Rachel Reed**

director of design & production, **Troy Look**

graphic designer, **Hilary Thompson**

digital prepress technician, **Angie Dobson**

managing editor, **Ari Yarwood**

senior editor, **Charlie Chu**

editor, **Robin Herrera**

editorial assistant, **Bess Pallares**

director of logistics, **Brad Rooks**

logistics associate, **Jung Lee**

onipress.com
facebook.com/onipress
twitter.com/onipress
onipress.tumblr.com
instagram.com/onipress
badmachinery.com

FIRST EDITION: MARCH 2017

ISBN 978-1-62010-387-6
EISBN 978-1-62010-097-4

PRINTED IN CHINA.

LIBRARY OF CONGRESS CONTROL NUMBER: 2016955405

1 2 3 4 5 6 7 8 9 10

The Case of The Team Spirit

Shauna Wickle

"Today might be the first day of a troubled adolescence."

Sonny Craven

"Mr. Bough has 'surprise picnic' written all over him."

Mildred Haversham

"Fight them like you do when you see something in a bin that looks tasty."

Charlotte Grote

"Messin' with people's reality is my special skill."

Linton Baxter

"At times like this you have to get behind the team."

Jack Finch

"If she's not running after you with a mop handle, you aren't trying."

GLOSSARY

I am given to understand (hem hem) that this book may be read around the world. To assist my new, international friends, here is a list of the words, phrases and concepts used in the book what you might find well alien and weird. I've explained them pretty well, I think you will find.

LOVE,
Charlotte
XXX

Big School: There are two "tiers" to the UK education system, 4-11 and 11-16 or 18 if you hang around. Really it should be tears not tiers because you are gonna know terror at how much bigger kids can be than you. Middle schools were tried but considered "too nice" and "weakening to the mind."

Plops: "manure" is the polite way to say it maybe?

Rugby School: A school where they play rugby not soccer-style football. Schools what put on airs and graces. Flipping heck it is just running around with balls, get over yourselves.

Cricket: Mystifying game where even fans do not understand most rules and games can last five days. More polite than other sports?

The Velvet Underground: The most frightening group of musical people ever assembled. Recruited from prison or so I heard.

Nuffink: The way you say "nothing" if you were dragged up rather than brought up.

WORR: Just a sound you make when something is pretty good. Very versatile I would say. (Also "worrrrr" or "wor".)

Lithium: A sort of metal that cheers you up I think? You probably shouldn't eat it raw.

Zine: A magazine that under normal circumstances would not be considered good enough to a. read or b. buy but people persist anyway because it is fun.

Pie: In Great Britain pies are usually savoury, it is just our way, we eat the other kind but only on special occasions e.g. Queen's birthday, national whipped cream surplus.

Diggers: Those yellow trucks with an arm that digs deep holes in the living earth, what are you, two years old? Keep up.

Football Ground: The stadium. A big old waste of seats and grass if you ask me but I suppose that you aren't (asking) so never mind.

Mutually Assured Mutual Conference Division 2: The football league tables in England are named and numbered in such a way as to keep newcomers to the game guessing. The selection of a cryptic sponsor really helps the process. The top league should be called something like "the Premierity", then the second one is "the Deluxe Parade" and then the third is "Division One" and the fourth perhaps "Stage Two (North)". Remember, they are just kicking an old ball about. They have to dress it up or no one would show up to watch.

Dribble: Drool. Also, kick an old ball about.

Local Newspaper: Newspaper about your town, telling you how a local man stole four bags of charcoal from a supermarket.

Brass Monkeys: The full phrase is that it is "cold enough to freeze the balls off a brass monkey", but that is pretty rude you will agree. The vicar would not like it.

Sorreh: The way you say "sorry" if you were dragged up rather than brought up.

The Milk Cup: Apparently people in the 1980s were so bored of football that it had to be sponsored by the second least interesting drink (after water.) This really happened.

The lads played their hearts out: Football men have special phrases they are taught to say on television because they didn't pay any attention in school. This is the best one. If they really played their hearts out, they would all be in hospital.

Biscuit: What you have at four o'clock with your tea slash coffee drink. Like a cookie invented in a world without luxury. Different from the American biscuit which is a savoury scone that has been drowned in gravy for its crimes.

Buffers: The very old.

Pudding: Dessert. The most important meal of the day.

Bursting: Piddle crisis point.

Tackleford City is a club with a history reaching back more than 100 years. For the last century, City have prided themselves on "football played the right way."

Many players have passed through the club, not to mention managers, coaches, team doctors, bus drivers, ball boys, groundskeepers, board members and kit-men. But the most important people to pass through the great gates of the Fig Roll Stadium (previously Wasp's Nest Cottage) are you, the fans.

In this brief guide, it was necessary to miss out many moments that fans will remember fondly. But in the space allowed, we've tried to bring you the pivotal events that have made this football club famous and beloved world-wide.

Written in the news clippings collected here are the foundation stones of "a gilded history". I certainly enjoyed my trip down "memory lane", and I hope you do too! I'm proud to have played for, managed, and eventually provided janitorial services for, the greatest club on earth.

Brian Nuttall
October 2009

October 4, 1912

Association football finally comes to Tackleford

FOLLOWING A RELAXATION of the strict town by-laws, the newly formed Tackleford City Association Football Club played their first ever home game this afternoon, an exhibition match against Pendlebury & Rasmond Colliery.

The match was a 5-5 tie, with Reggie Dimmock bagging all five for the visitors and Jimmy Brett, Walpole McGinty (2) and Edgar Storch (2) replying for Tackleford.

This first match for the city's newly-formed football club was cause for great celebration in the pubs and cafés of Tackleford. Men and women, boys and girls poured out onto the streets, keen to see the game played at last by local lads. Due to the enthusiastic haste with which the game had been arranged, no "pitch" had been secured, so the match was played in the ancient style, with stone goalmouths erected at the city's most northerly and southerly points.

While the initial passages of the game were chaotic, and goals looked unlikely, the locals (and a large travelling contingent from Pendlebury) aligned themselves with the teams, swelling each to around 75 men, and the match was played along the two miles of Main Street for four and three-quarter hours.

Pendlebury & Rasmond coach Ted Bentham declared the game "the stuff of great human endeavour," over meat pies and gravy served at St Austwick's church that evening.

July 18, 1915

First match at Wasp's Nest

HAVING PLAYED THEIR first season in the Second Division on marshland, Tackleford City finally have a purpose-built stadium from which to launch their aspirations to top-flight association football.

But the move to the luxurious new Wasp's Nest Cottage ground, paid for by the City Trust, has not proved popular with the players, many of whom preferred the club's previous home on the marshes.

"Teams didn't like playing us on the marshes," said centre-back Humbert Jones. "While it was difficult to play on that surface, we were used to it. Once you'd learned where the quagmires and water pits were, you could play around them."

"We could usually rely on the opposition losing at least a couple of players to broken legs or trench foot."

It was the disappearance of Wanderers and England outside-right Walter Hayes during a particularly foggy night game that lead Tackleford City to abandon their home on Hamble Moor. The new ground will provide terraced standing for 30,000 and offer top-line health and training facilities to the team.

"We're leading the way in cleanliness," said City Trust chairman Alan Gough. "Dirt is the number one cause of goals conceded. If a player is caked in filth, how can his team-mates tell who they're playing to?"

To that end, a 13-man bath, the first of its kind, has been installed in a purpose-built hut behind the stands. Bars of soap have been provided by local disinfectant manufacturer Wallis Hornbeam & Sons, and the local Women's Institute have supplied monogrammed towels for all first team players.

April 26, 1924

"Fabulous Swami" proves too much for Sunderland

VISITORS SUNDERLAND were put to the sword on Saturday after a virtuoso performance by Tackleford City in the FA Cup Final.

Sunderland, unbeaten in 21 games, started the game well, but proved no match for Empire signing Sanjay Rhamaswami, whose unconventional playing style helped City secure a 4-0 win.

"Swami", hailed by City manager Bert Best as "a decent enough fellow once you spend time with him," astonished the opposing team by floating over the pitch, shooting an eerie green ray from an emerald on his turban, vanishing only to appear on a completely different part of the pitch moments later, and scoring a penalty in the 54th minute following a goalmouth foul on City full-back Paul Barrington.

City's other goals came from Don Hardwyck, Dennis Andrews and Mr Watson. Sunderland's best chance came when their star forward Bob Kelly broke through City's defence, but he was distracted by Swami's suddenly red, glowing eyes, and failed to convert the opportunity.

Sunderland chairman Lord Sunderland is understood to be asking for a replay. "These foreign footballers are spoiling the game. Sooner or later the rules of association football must be written down somewhere."

March 19, 1942

Makeshift player makes fine debut

AS THE WAR IN Europe and beyond drags on, Tackleford City's participation in the Northern League has been continually hampered by lack of manpower, with most able-bodied men stationed abroad fighting the Axis powers.

However, Bulldog Bobby spirit and good old British innovation were to the fore as City introduced their newest recruit, "Rufus X-15", an entirely mechanical player constructed from reclaimed crashed aeroplane parts.

"Rufus may represent the future of the game," said interim City coach Don Dickens. "He only needs a quart of petrol and a squeeze of oil and he'll run for 90 minutes."

Dickens, whose dropped arches and fancy ways made him unsuitable for service in battle, has made his name with a series of innovations on and off the pitch. Wasp's Nest Cottage is the only stadium in the country with radar, ground-to-air munitions, and a cannon generating thick fog should enemies strike from the air.

Rufus X-15 put an astonishing eight goals past Hardwycke FC keeper Ken Best in an 8-0 thrashing that saw City go second in the league, with a game in hand. "He moved so fast," said Best, "his legs were like pistons. In that they were actually driven by pistons. He really kept me on my toes."

A visiting Mr Churchill described the mechanical man as "queer, but oddly exciting."

April 30, 1953

Nuttall's men are champions

A LAST MINUTE header by Ken Toblowsky secured the Division One championship for Tackleford City on the final day of the season, taking them ahead of defending champions Rye Athletic on goal difference.

Player-manager Brian Nuttall, who replaced the late Austin Mansfield as team boss mid-season, put the late run down to "grit and heart." The team's victory may also be due to the return of Rufus X-15, discovered in a caretaker's cupboard below the Whittaker Stand, covered in rust and cobwebs.

"There's no discounting Rufus X-15's 61 goals in nine games," said Nuttall, "but this is the story of eleven men, not one man who isn't actually a man, technically speaking."

Nuttall was reluctant to discuss the tin player's fortunes, adding that the wartime hero had "seen better days," and would probably "be sent to the knacker's yard or sold for scrap."

February 1, 1964

Alpine disaster claims keeper

RELIEF AT THE recovery from an avalanche of the train carrying the Tackleford City team in the Alps was tinged with heartbreak, when it was discovered that goalkeeper Lawrence "Fatty" Vickers had died during the week that the locomotive was lost.

"After supplies in the buffet car were exhausted, starvation drove us half-mad," said striker Neil Bosson. "We came together and made a decision. There was more eating on Fatty than on the rest of us put together."

"The choice was simple. Either we ate Fatty, or we ate four other people."

Vickers, who had played for City since 1961/62 and had 8 caps for England, was known for his cat-like agility, far greater than that of other men of his size. He is survived by his wife and six children. Fatty will be replaced in goal on Saturday by reserve keeper "Tiny" Tom Lane.

IN THE NEWS

• Following the war, where regional leagues replaced the usual programme, football got back into its swing with the 1946/7 season. After nearly six years of national unity, many men found it difficult to engage each other in competition. 91% of games in the first post-war season ended in goalless draws.

• There were many innovations in the game during the fifties, and few were more controversial than the "kit wars" of 1958/59. Exploiting lax regulations, teams turned out in ever more outrageous couture, often inspired by the fashions of Paris and Milan. The Football Association stepped in after Leeds Utd took to the pitch for a league cup tie in tin foil dungarees and berets.

• Mechanical player Rufus X-15 was one of the most intriguing figures of the era. He escaped to Switzerland in May 1953 where he managed Neuchâtel Xamax for six successful seasons.

May 1, 1975

Sir Ron steers City to their historic "quadruple" in Milan

AFTER NEARLY TWO decades in the doldrums, few could have predicted that, following a win in the league championship and triumphs in both League and FA Cups, Tackleford City would cap their season with a 4-2 victory over Paris St Germain in the Fairs Cup.

The night was marred in places by City's "tactics", which involved a kind of fierce physicality rarely exercised by teams on the continent.

PSG were unable to play their usual skilful passing game under a volley of sliding tackles, hard-headed jostling, robust language and energetic two-man challenges. After creating an early two-goal lead through Michel Dugarry and Jean le Coq, they wilted under City's relentless pressure and capitulated to quick-fire goals by Smith, Smith, Smith and Susan. The French side struggled after their goalkeeper Leon Potiche fell down a set of stairs at half-time.

Manager Ron Ramsay made no apology after the match for his team's uncompromising style.

"We're not here to play like a bunch of fairies at a tea party," he said. "We're here to win games. If the French don't like it, they're welcome to complain. I doubt anyone will be listening to them carping on."

An open-top bus parade of Tackleford city centre is planned for Friday.

The most feared team of the mid-seventies, in their pomp

October 4, 1978

Ramsay's rein ends after 30 "awful" days

JUST A MONTH after departing Tackleford to become England manager, Ron Ramsay has quit to take up a role as national coach of oil-rich football newcomers Saudi Arabia.

"The move has nothing to do with money," said Ramsay, rumoured to be receiving a golden palace and an obsidian limousine alongside a £1 million-per-year salary. "England are an unmanageable team."

Ramsay, who lead City to nine trophies in four years, declared the England players "an utter shambles" to reporters from all over the world at a press conference in Jeddah.

"Modern players are more interested in combing their hair than they are winning games," he blasted, "they'd rather be appearing on tea-time television than mastering performing a roundhouse kick while the referee's back is turned."

"Kenny Jones might be the most talented dribbler of the ball since the days of Arthur Clackett, but he's no idea how to snap another man's cruciate ligament during a mid-air fight for the ball. Modern players just don't have it. I've had an awful time."

"The Saudis are going to change football overnight," he declared.

Dismissing the cream of English talent as "a shower, a pathetic shower," Ramsay departed the press conference throwing gold coins at the assembled reporters, before being sped away by two sheiks wearing sunglasses.

March 28, 1985

Plucky Tackleford steal Milk Cup from Totley Town

A DECADE AFTER they won four trophies in the famous "quadruple season", Tackleford City finally have a new piece of silverware on the shelf.

An extra-time goal from Norman Cresswell secured a 3-2 League Cup Sponsored By Milk win for a side whose fortunes have greatly diminished since their days as the powerhouse of English football in the mid-seventies.

The board's refusal to replace Ron Ramsay lead to three successive relegations from 1979 to 1981, with a new manager only being sought as the team faced ejection from the league in the spring of 1982. Then-chairman Ted Spofforth notoriously turned up for work in pyjamas and slippers for months at a time, becoming renowned for crying during board meetings.

Fans, bereft at the loss of their iconic manager, took to wearing black and refused to celebrate the scoring of goals, often turning their backs on the pitch and sobbing.

It was only a new generation of players, all of whom were drawn from outside the club's grief-stricken youth team, who managed to save the club from vanishing altogether.

"There's a new spirit at the club," said Cresswell. "If the gaffer sees anyone weeping uncontrollably in the dressing room, we whips them with a wet towel. Things are looking up."

August 16, 1994

"Team of the nineties" powers back into top flight

AFTER COMING CLOSE to promotion over the last three years, Tackleford City begin their first Thompson's Menswear Premiership campaign at Finsbury Park FC today.

City will be the last team promoted using the controversial "montessori system", which was abandoned at the end of the last season.

The complicated formula combining matches won and drawn, goal difference, charitable work, player politeness and a written examination was introduced in 1992 by European football chiefs, but produced some very unreliable results.

Clubs complained that the ability to factor in the chart position of pop recordings made by first team players encouraged sides to spend too long in the recording studio. City midfielder Carl Patterson's "Baby, I Think I'm In Love With You" spent two months in the singles top ten in March, easing Tackleford back into football's elite.

"Carl's disappointed that his golden throat can't help the lads any more," said manager Brian Bassett. "But he's going to keep working on his songs. He's excited about making music."

July 11, 2007

Chastened City face bankruptcy

AFTER EIGHT YEARS of wild, profligate spending, Tackleford City were declared bankrupt today.

Citing ever-rising wage bills, the failure of expensive £20 million transfers Luciano Bosma from FC Dubrovnik and Terry Timms from Grimethorpe, City were issued with a winding-up order by administrators at 10am today.

Investors heard how a culture of lavish parties, with caviar, dwarves on horseback, witch doctors, high-kicking chorus girls and moustachio'd sharpshooters, had drained the northern club's cash reserves.

"We've made mistakes," said outgoing chairman Rod Wainwright. "But we had a good time. Good lord, we had one hell of a good time."

IN THE NEWS

• After the hooliganism and violence of the 1980s, football got back on its feet in the nineties. Billionaire team owners like Sir Ledley Egg (Peckham Forest), Dame Lucille le Havre (Cheshunt Rangers) and Henry Fox (FC Yorkshire Force) pushed player prices - and attendances - ever higher with their deep pockets. le Havre was frowned upon for "buying the title" in 1994, but the league championship has now not been held by a traditional "pauper" team since Wrexham Rovers triumphed in 1996/7.

• The influx of cash into football meant that many foreign superstars were lured to England's shores by the promise of gold. Not all of them proved successful. Signed by league-leaders Harrogate West FC, Spanish striker Juan Costas ended his debut season living in a caravan in his club's car park.

• In 1999, the Queen's horse was allowed into Wembley for the FA Cup Final. This proved to be a very costly and dangerous mistake.

August 9, 2007

New owner: "trophies or else" for City

NEW OWNER YURI Kropotkin, who bought Tackleford City for £1 this morning, has set his sights on "trophies or else" in the new season.

"This is a family club, but the team must play well. If they do not, I fire them, get new team. Manager fails, I fire him, get new manager. No one is safe. We must win all the cups."

However, despite City's slide into financial ruin, billionaire Kropotkin sees no reason to rein in the organisation's more flamboyant side.

"Caviar, dwarves on horseback, witch doctors, high-kicking chorus girls and moustachio'd sharpshooters are all welcome here. Man is on earth for only short time. It must be a good time. Otherwise why live at all?"

"Our lads will win on the pitch by day and spend their nights in luxurious ecstacy. It is only right."

JOHN ALLISON

Born in a hidden village deep within the British Alps, John Allison came into this world a respectable baby with style and taste. Having been exposed to American comics at an early age, he spent decades honing his keen mind and his massive body in order to burn out this colonial cultural infection.

One of the longest continuously publishing independent web-based cartoonists, John has plied his trade since the late nineties moving from *Bobbins* to *Scary Go Round* to *Bad Machinery,* developing the deeply weird world of Tackleford long after many of his fellow artists were ground into dust and bones by Time Itself.

He has only once shed a single tear, but you only meet Sergio Aragonés for the first time once.

John resides in Letchworth Garden City, England and is known to his fellow villagers only as He Who Has Conquered.

—Contributed by Richard Stevens III

"THE TREASURE OF BRITANNIA"

BAD MACHINERY, VOLUME 2:
THE CASE OF THE GOOD BOY
By John Allison
ISBN 978-1-62010-114-8
Pocket Edition Coming Fall 2017!

BAD MACHINERY, VOLUME 3:
THE CASE OF THE SIMPLE SOUL
By John Allison
ISBN 978-1-62010-193-3
Pocket Edition Coming Spring 2018!

BAD MACHINERY, VOLUME 4:
THE CASE OF THE LONELY ONE
By John Allison
ISBN 978-1-62010-212-1
Pocket Edition Coming Fall 2018!

BAD MACHINERY, VOLUME 5:
THE CASE OF THE FIRE INSIDE
By John Allison
ISBN 978-1-62010-297-8
Pocket Edition Coming Spring 2019!

BAD MACHINERY, VOLUME 6:
THE CASE OF THE UNWELCOME VISITOR
By John Allison
ISBN 978-1-62010-351-7
Pocket Edition Coming Fall 2019!

BAD MACHINERY, VOL. 7:
THE CASE OF THE FORKED ROAD
By John Allison
ISBN 978-1-62010-390-6
First edition available May 2017!

FOR MORE INFORMATION ON THESE AND OTHER FINE ONI PRESS COMIC BOOKS AND GRAPHIC NOVELS VISIT WWW.ONIPRESS.COM. TO FIND A COMIC SPECIALTY STORE IN YOUR AREA VISIT WWW.COMICSHOPS.US.

ONI PRESS
www.onipress.com